TULSA CITY-COUNTY LIBRARY

damage
Noted
M80/HR2
07/15/24

SPACE TECH
ROCKETS

by Allan Morey

BELLWETHER MEDIA • MINNEAPOLIS, MN

EPIC BOOKS are no ordinary books. They burst with intense action, high-speed heroics, and shadows of the unknown. Are you ready for an Epic adventure?

This edition first published in 2018 by Bellwether Media, Inc.

No part of this publication may be reproduced in whole or in part without written permission of the publisher. For information regarding permission, write to Bellwether Media, Inc., Attention: Permissions Department, 5357 Penn Avenue South, Minneapolis, MN 55419.

Library of Congress Cataloging-in-Publication Data

Names: Morey, Allan.
Title: Rockets / by Allan Morey.
Description: Minneapolis, MN : Bellwether Media, Inc., 2018. | Series: Epic.
  Space tech | Audience: Ages 7-12. | Includes bibliographical references and index.
Identifiers: LCCN 2016059027 (print) | LCCN 2017016291 (ebook) | ISBN 9781626177055 (hardcover : alk. paper) | ISBN 9781681034355 (ebook) | ISBN 9781618912886 (paperback : alk. paper)
Subjects: LCSH: Rockets (Aeronautics)–Juvenile literature. | Outer space–Exploration–Juvenile literature.
Classification: LCC TL782.5 (ebook) | LGC TL782.5 .M64 2018 (print) | DDC 629.47/5 |2 23
LC record available at https://lccn.loc.gov/2016059027

Text copyright © 2018 by Bellwether Media, Inc. EPIC BOOKS and associated logos are trademarks and/or registered trademarks of Bellwether Media, Inc. SCHOLASTIC, CHILDREN'S PRESS, and associated logos are trademarks and/or registered trademarks of Scholastic Inc., 557 Broadway, New York, NY 10012.

Editor: Nathan Sommer   Designer: Steve Porter

Printed in the United States of America, North Mankato, MN.

TABLE OF CONTENTS

ROCKET AT WORK! 4
WHAT ARE ROCKETS? 6
PARTS OF ROCKETS 8
ROCKET MISSIONS 14
SPACE LAUNCH SYSTEM SPECS 20
GLOSSARY 22
TO LEARN MORE 23
INDEX 24

ROCKET AT WORK!

A crowd gathers to watch the takeoff of a new rocket. The countdown begins. Engines roar. Then Falcon 9 blasts off into space!

FLYING AGAIN!

The Falcon 9 is one of the first rockets that can be used more than once.

Falcon 9

It carries a **spacecraft** that will deliver supplies to the **International Space Station**.

WHAT ARE ROCKETS?

Rockets are powerful spacecraft. They are needed to push things beyond Earth. Some carry supplies or **space shuttles**. Others lift unmanned machines like **satellites**.

rocket launching a satellite

space shuttle

PARTS OF ROCKETS

Rockets have tall, thin frames. Their shape helps them cut through the air. Powerful engines shoot gas down. Then the rockets blast up.

BLAST OFF!
Rockets leave Earth at 7 miles (11 kilometers) per second!

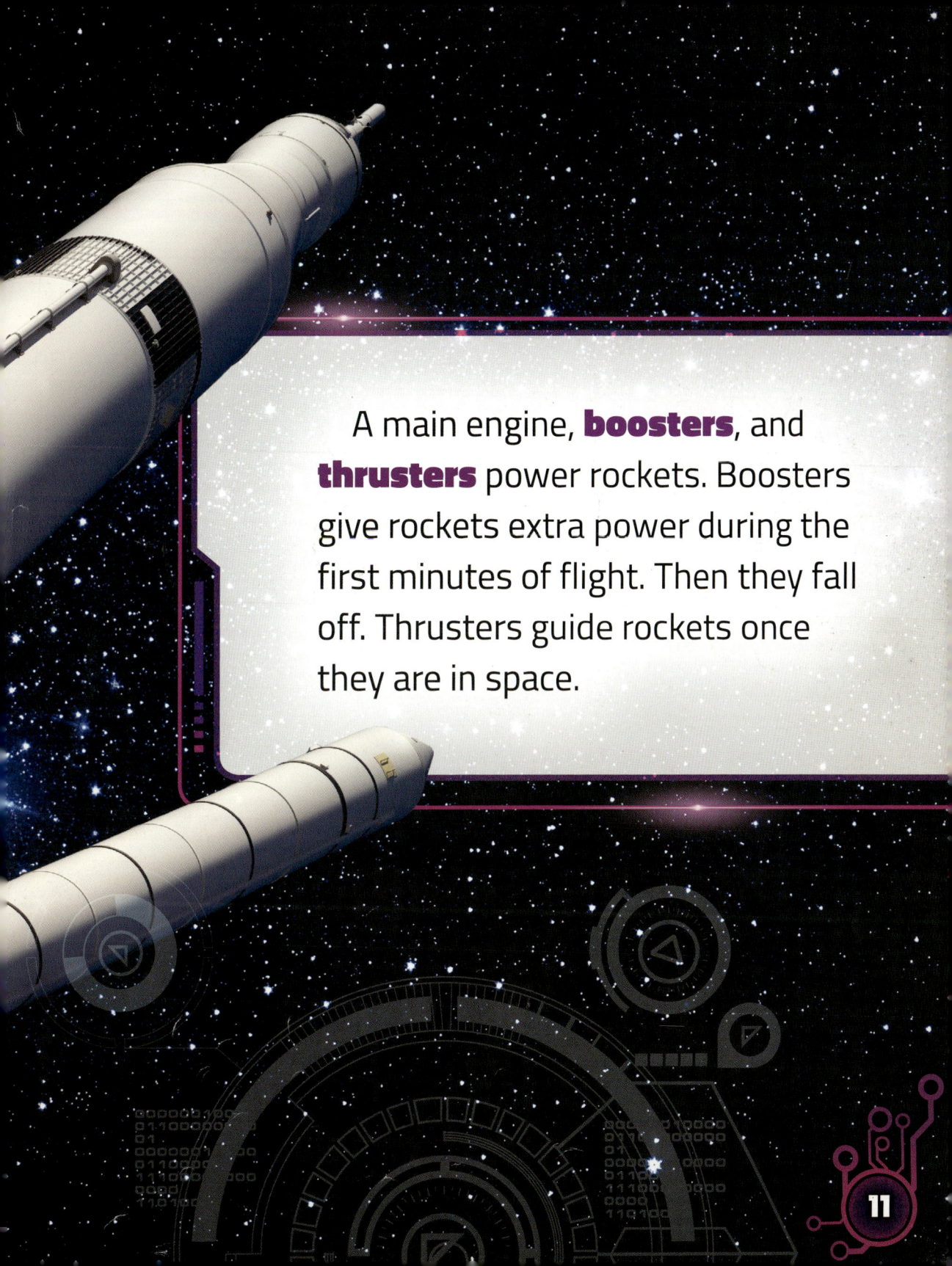

A main engine, **boosters**, and **thrusters** power rockets. Boosters give rockets extra power during the first minutes of flight. Then they fall off. Thrusters guide rockets once they are in space.

The top part of a rocket holds supplies or **astronauts**. The middle part has a **guidance system**. This holds computers that tell the rocket where to go. The bottom part usually has fins to help the rocket fly straight.

astronaut

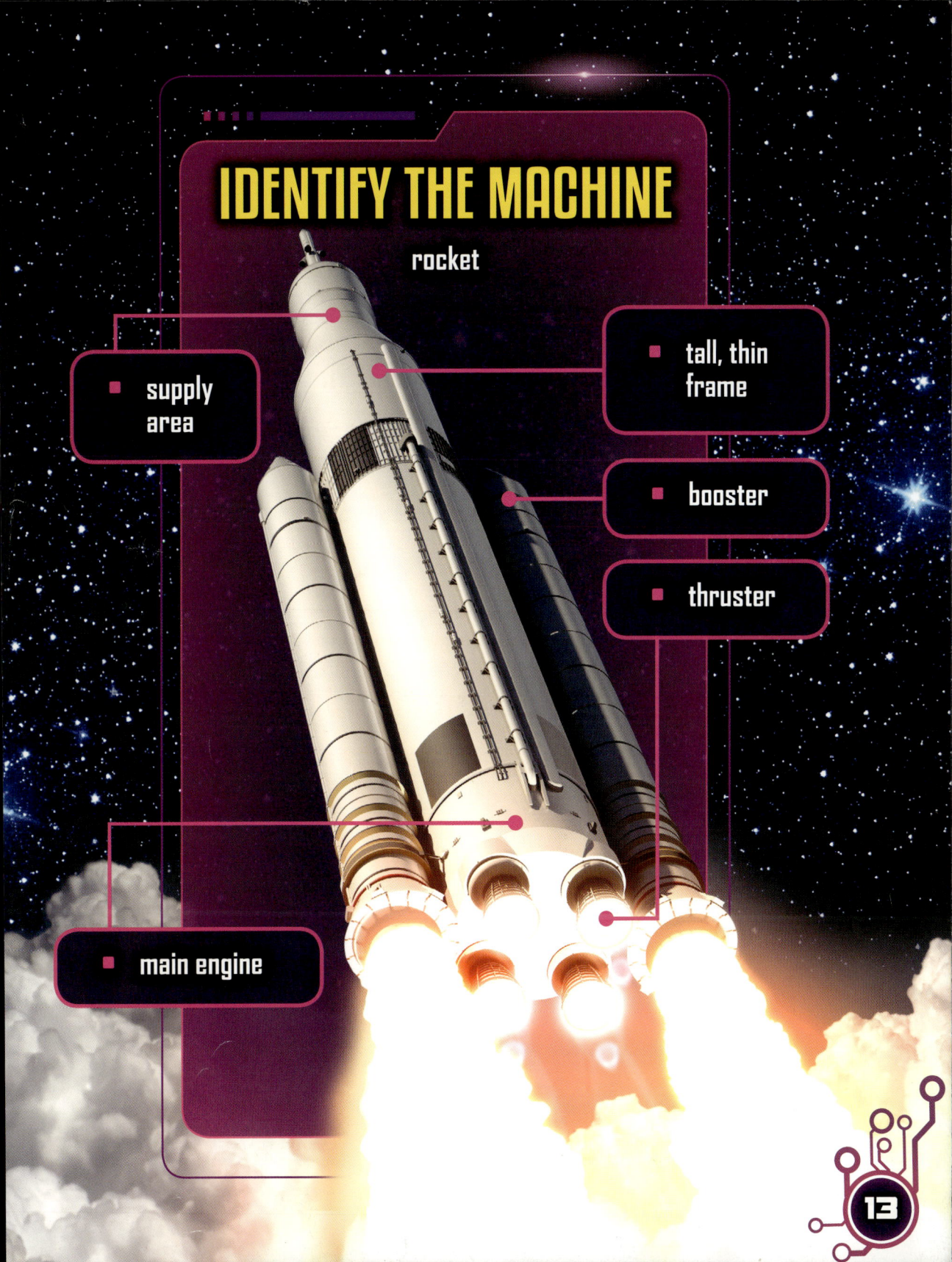

IDENTIFY THE MACHINE

rocket

- supply area
- tall, thin frame
- booster
- thruster
- main engine

13

ROCKET MISSIONS

The **Soviet Union** was the first country to use space rockets. It used a rocket to carry the first satellite into **orbit** in 1957. The Saturn V rocket from **NASA** helped humans reach the moon in 1969!

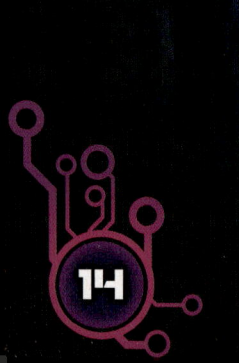

Sputnik 1, first satellite

ROCKET POWER!

At its launch, the Saturn V rocket was the most powerful space rocket ever used successfully. It weighed as much as about 400 elephants!

Rockets have been used for every space **mission**. From 1981 to 2011, rockets lifted space shuttles into orbit. Recently, they have been used to send machines to Mars.

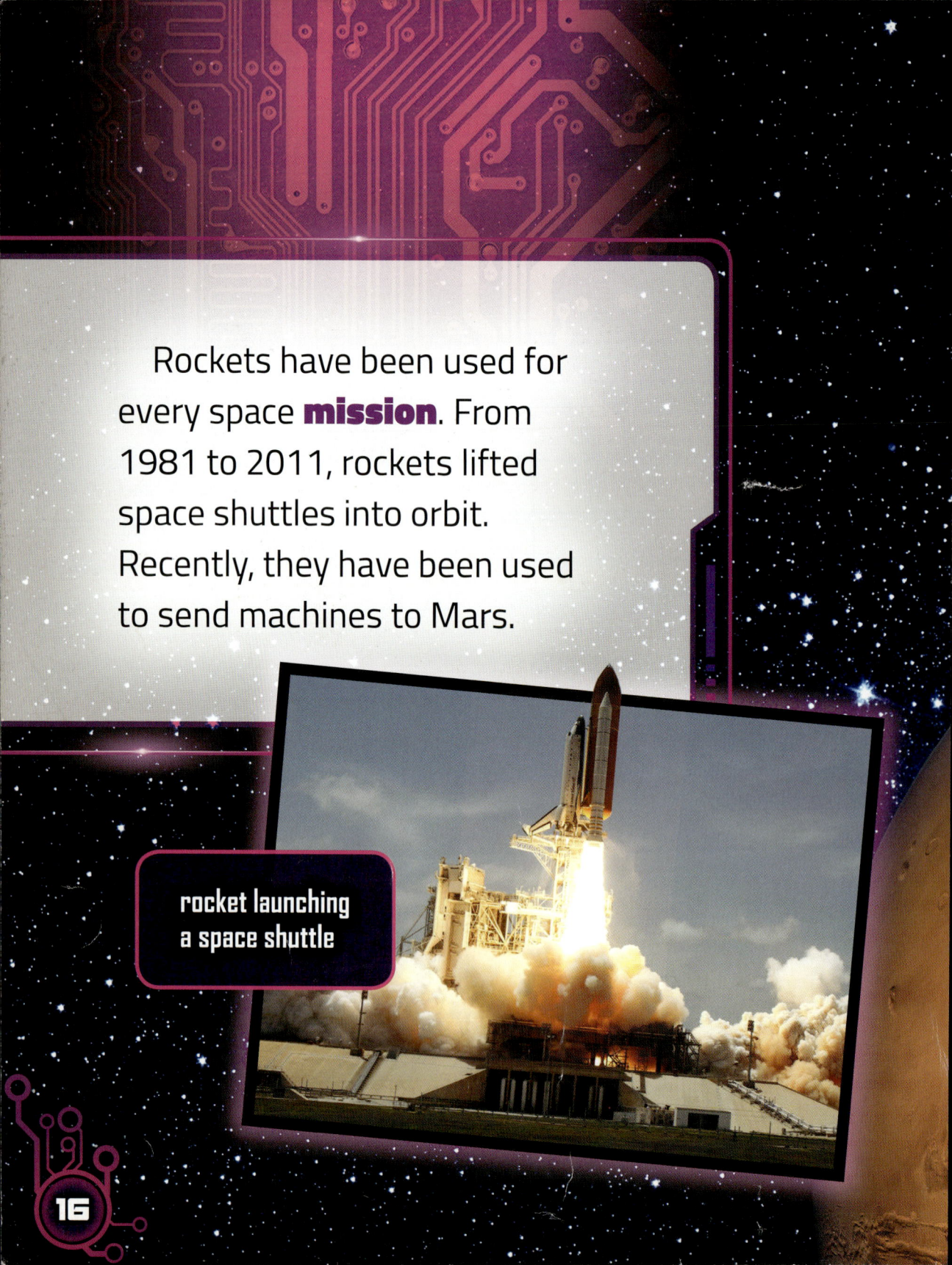

rocket launching a space shuttle

satellite orbiting Mars

SPEED DEMONS!

Many rockets must travel 25 times faster than the speed of sound to reach Earth's orbit.

NASA continues to build even more powerful rockets. Its Space Launch System (SLS) rocket can reach **deep space**. It may even be used to send humans to Mars. Without rockets, visiting space would be very hard!

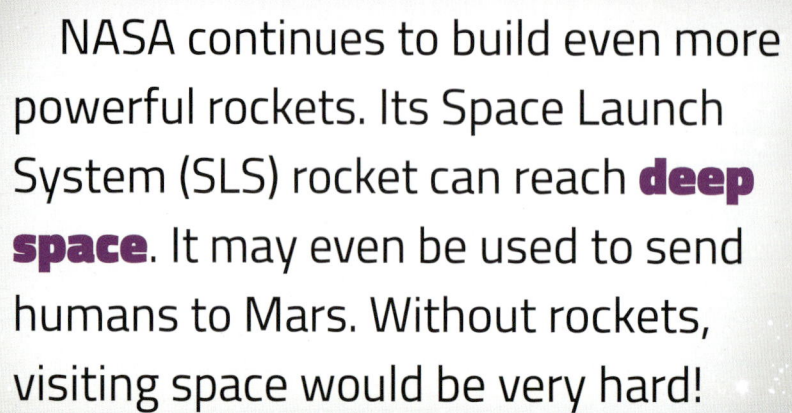

Mars and its two moons

Space Launch System rocket

SPACE LAUNCH SYSTEM SPECS

TEST ROCKET!

NASA uses a model of the SLS to test the rocket at high speeds.

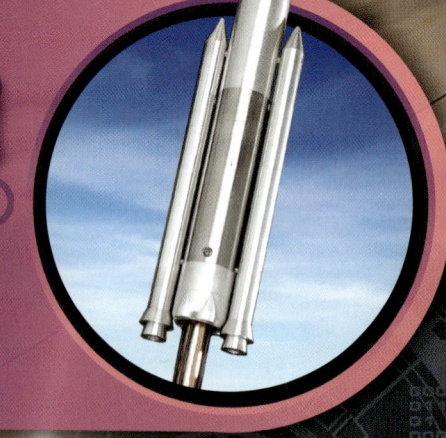

NAME: SLS
Space Launch System - Block 1

- **missions:** to send humans, supplies, and machines beyond Earth's orbit; to help astronauts eventually reach Mars and asteroids

- **weight at liftoff:** 2,875 tons (2,608 metric tons)

- **first time in space:** planned for 2019

- **location in space:** anywhere beyond Earth's orbit

- **height:** 322 feet (98 meters)

- **width:** 27.6 feet (8.4 meters) in diameter

21

GLOSSARY

astronauts—people trained to travel and work in outer space

boosters—rocket parts that add power to aid in takeoff

deep space—any part of space beyond the moon's orbit around Earth

guidance system—a system that controls the movement of a spacecraft

International Space Station—a place for astronauts from all over the world to work in outer space

mission—a task or job

NASA—National Aeronautics and Space Administration; NASA is a U.S. government agency responsible for space travel and exploration.

orbit—to circle around an object

satellites—objects in space that orbit a larger object

Soviet Union—a former country in eastern Europe and western Asia made up of 15 smaller republics or states

space shuttles—reusable spacecraft that carry people and cargo between Earth and outer space

spacecraft—any vehicle used to travel in outer space

thrusters—small engines on a spacecraft used to control its direction in outer space

TO LEARN MORE

AT THE LIBRARY

Baker, David, and Heather Kissock. *Rockets*. New York, N.Y.: AV2 by Weigl, 2017.

Linde, Barbara M. *Rocket Scientists*. New York, N.Y.: PowerKids Press, 2016.

VanVoorst, Jenny Fretland. *Rockets*. Minneapolis, Minn.: Pogo, 2017.

ON THE WEB

Learning more about rockets is as easy as 1, 2, 3.

1. Go to www.factsurfer.com.

2. Enter "rockets" into the search box.

3. Click the "Surf" button and you will see a list of related web sites.

With factsurfer.com, finding more information is just a click away.

INDEX

astronauts, 12, 21

boosters, 10, 11, 13

deep space, 18

Earth, 6, 8, 17, 21

engines, 4, 8, 11, 13

Falcon 9 rocket, 4, 5

fins, 12

frames, 8, 13

guidance system, 12

Identify the Machine, 13

International Space Station, 5

Mars, 16, 17, 18, 21

mission, 16, 21

moon, 14, 18

NASA, 14, 18, 20

orbit, 14, 16, 17, 21

satellites, 6, 14, 15, 17

Saturn V rocket, 14, 15

Soviet Union, 14

Space Launch System, 18, 19, 20, 21

space shuttles, 6, 7, 16

spacecraft, 5, 6

specs, 21

speed, 8, 17, 20

Sputnik 1 satellite, 14, 15

supplies, 5, 6, 12, 13, 21

thrusters, 10, 11, 13

The images in this book are reproduced through the courtesy of: 3Dsculptor, front cover, pp. 6 (framed rocket), 8-11 (all), 13 (rocket), 17 (rocket-FunFact), 18-19 (SLS launch); Aphelleon, pp. 2-3; NASA, pp. 4-5 (all), 6-7, 12 (framed astronaut), 12-13 (Earth), 15 (rocket-FunFact), 16 (framed shuttle launch), 17 (satellite), 18 (framed Mars), 20 (rocket model-FunFact), 21 (SLS rocket); Petrovich9/ NASA, p. 8 (rocket-FunFact); xtock, p. 8 (Earth-FunFact); Vadim Sadovski, p. 14 (Earth/moon); FreshPaint, pp. 14-15 (Sputnik 1); Tristan3D, pp. 16-17 (Mars); CHAIWATPHOTOS, p. 20 (sky-FunFact); United Launch Alliance, pp. 20-21.